Secret Kingdom

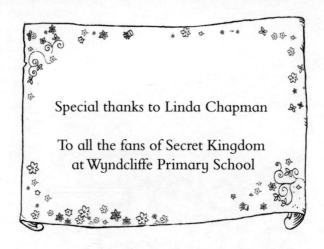

Special thanks to Linda Chapman

To all the fans of Secret Kingdom
at Wyndcliffe Primary School

ORCHARD BOOKS

First published in Great Britain in 2014 by Orchard Books
This edition published in 2017 by The Watts Publishing Group

1 3 5 6 7 9 10 8 6 4 2

A CIP catalogue record for this book is available from the British Library.

ISBN 978 1 40835 299 1

Printed in Great Britain by Clays Ltd, St Ives plc

Orchard Books
An imprint of Hachette Children's Group
Part of The Watts Publishing Group Limited
Carmelite House, 50 Victoria Embankment, London EC4Y 0DZ

An Hachette UK Company
www.hachette.co.uk
www.hachettechildrens.co.uk

Series created by Hothouse Fiction
www.hothousefiction.com

Sapphire Spell

ROSIE BANKS

ORCHARD

This is the Secret Kingdom

Sapphire Stream

Contents

Summer's Birthday

Summer Hammond stood very still and held out a handful of animal food. The two deer came close to the fence and snuffled at her hand. Their eyes were like forest pools – deep and dark. Summer grinned as she reached out and stroked their velvety noses. She thought they were beautiful – but then she loved all animals, even spiders!

"Smile!" Jasmine called out from behind her. Summer turned and grinned as Jasmine quickly took a couple of photos.

"Don't move for a second!" Ellie called from where she was crouching down on the grass, drawing a quick picture of the deer in her notebook. She loved to draw and always carried a notebook and pen around with her. She drew a few more lines and then carefully tore the page out. "Happy Birthday!" she said, offering it to Summer with a smile.

Summer gave the deer one last pat and went over to see the drawing. It was brilliant. It completely captured the gorgeous animals – and her huge grin! "Thank you!" Summer hugged Ellie. "This is just the best way to spend my birthday – at Honeyvale Wildlife Park with my two best friends and lots of animals!" she declared.

They all smiled at each other.

"I love it here too," said Jasmine. "All the different animals give me ideas for dance steps. Look, this is how a squirrel moves…" She ran with short, light steps and hid behind a tree, popping her head out. "And this is a deer." She leaped into the air, throwing her head and arms back.

Ellie stuffed her notebook into her

backpack and grinned. "And this is a rabbit!" She crouched down and did some bunny hops before tripping over a tree root and landing on her tummy.

"A very clumsy rabbit!" Summer giggled. The deer skittered away, bounding gracefully into the trees.

Their movement stirred a memory in Summer's mind. "Do you remember the magic reindeer we met in the Secret Kingdom?" she asked her friends. "They were even more beautiful than these deer."

"Oh yes," said Ellie dreamily. "And they could fly!"

The Secret Kingdom was an amazing land that only they knew about. It was a beautiful place that was usually ruled by kind, jolly King Merry. But recently something terrible had happened – his horrible sister, evil Queen Malice, had taken over! She had built a bridge into the Troll Territories and the trolls had helped her steal King Merry's crown and put him in a dungeon. The queen had declared herself the ruler of the Secret Kingdom and now everyone there had to do whatever she said.

"I wonder how poor King Merry is," Summer said anxiously.

Jasmine frowned. "I hate thinking of him being locked away in Thunder Castle."

"And everyone in the Secret Kingdom being so unhappy because of Queen Malice and the trolls," said Ellie. "Oh, I hope we can find the missing jewels!"

Jasmine and Summer nodded in agreement. Queen Malice couldn't be the *true* ruler of the Secret Kingdom until she had the four royal jewels that were always set into the ruler's crown – an emerald, a sapphire, a diamond and a ruby. King Merry had cast a spell to stop Queen Malice from stealing the jewels, but it had gone a bit wonky and now the little king had no idea where the precious jewels were hidden! If the girls could somehow find the jewels before Queen

Malice and bring them all together then a new crown would form and King Merry could rule again.

Summer, Ellie and Jasmine were desperate to help. They had already found one jewel – a beautiful green emerald – that had been hidden in Unicorn Valley. They wanted to go back and find the others, but they couldn't go and hunt for them until the finding spell in the Secret Spellbook had located where in the kingdom they were.

"I checked the spellbook this morning but the spell still wasn't finished," said Ellie, patting her backpack. She'd packed the spellbook in there to keep it safe.

"Maybe it'll have found one by now?" Jasmine said hopefully.

"Let's check!" Summer said. "It would

be the best birthday present ever to go and help the Secret Kingdom!"

Ellie glanced round. Summer's mum and step-dad were behind them, watching Summer's two little brothers, Finn and Connor, who were playing at being soldiers, crawling on their tummies through the grass and dry leaves. "OK. We'd better go somewhere else though. We don't want your family to see."

Summer nodded. The Secret Kingdom had to be kept secret! "Mum," she called. "We're going to go to the red-squirrel enclosure now. Is that all right?"

"OK," her mum replied. "Don't go too far ahead though."

"We won't," Summer promised.

They ran off down the woodland trail. When they were sure they were on their own they ducked behind a wooden bench at the side of the path.

Ellie undid her backpack and took out the spellbook and they all gasped. The cover of the old book was sparkling and glowing!

"I think the finding spell is ready!" said Jasmine excitedly.

Ellie crouched down and opened the book, flicking quickly though the old

pages until she got to the right place.

The finding spell was complete, and at the bottom of the page was a drawing of a beautiful blue stream surrounded by green rushes and trees. Fish jumped out of the water and butterflies and dragonflies danced through the air. Cute otters watched from the side.

Holding tightly onto the spellbook, Summer, Jasmine and Ellie read the words out together:

"Something's lost that must be found,
Search through sea, air and ground...
To the stream where water nymphs play
You must now find your way.
With the stone, all will be well
If you say this sapphire spell."

On the last word, the colour seemed to swirl out of the picture of the book, surrounding the girls and whisking them away. Jasmine held on tightly to the spellbook. They were bound to need it in the Secret Kingdom!

The girls spun round and round. At first they went too fast to see anything but gradually, like being on a roundabout,

they felt themselves slowing down as they spun and they could see the Secret Kingdom spread out beneath them.

Summer caught her breath. The land was normally so beautiful, with lush meadows, tall mountains, sandy beaches and glittering seas, but now it all looked dark and desolate. Instead of the wonderful creatures who lived there, all they could see were big, ugly trolls marching across the land with heavy clubs swinging in their hands.

The only bright spot was Unicorn Valley, where the girls had found the emerald. There the land was as beautiful as ever and unicorns were trotting and cantering through the grass happily. But the rest of the kingdom was a dreadful, gloomy sight.

"We have to find the jewels," shouted Jasmine fiercely. "We can't let Queen Malice do this to the Secret Kingdom!"

They started to spin down towards the ground. They could see a stream but it was nothing like the picture in the spellbook. It was dry and muddy and dirty, and beside it the trees and rushes were brown and dying. A big dam had been built across the water – a clumsy wall of wood and rocks. On the other side of the dam the stream had swollen into a big pool of beautiful blue water. The magic set them down right next to the dam.

As they landed, Ellie caught sight of their reflection and saw that they were all wearing their tiaras. Their tiaras magically appeared whenever they arrived in the kingdom to show people that they were special friends of King Merry, but ever since Queen Malice had taken over they had been dull and tarnished. Ellie sighed as she looked at hers. *We have to get King Merry his throne back and make everything right again!* she thought determinedly as she put the spellbook carefully away in her backpack.

"The spell talked about the sapphire, it must be here somewhere." Jasmine said. "And we're going to find it!"

Summer squeezed her friends' hands. She sometimes didn't feel quite as brave as the other two but she would do anything to help restore the Secret Kingdom to the happy, magical land it should be.

"I wonder who built this dam," she said, looking at the trickle of muddy water in the river bed. "The stream this side is drying up because of it."

"There's a notice," Jasmine realised. "Over there!" She pointed to a large sign with blackened spiky edges. She clambered across the reeds and went over to look at it.

"ROYAL BATHING LAKE: KEEP OUT!" she read aloud.

The girls looked at each other. "Queen

Malice," said Ellie grimly.

Just then there was a rustle in the big clump of bulrushes beside them. Summer jumped in surprise. "What's that?"

Jasmine stepped towards the noise. "Come out!" she shouted bravely. "Come out right now, whoever you are!"

The Secret Clearing

A little furry otter poked its head out of
the rushes. The girls breathed a sigh of
relief as he came gambolling towards
them, hopping over the brown, dry reeds
in the empty river bed. He bounded
over to Summer and she crouched down
to stroke his sleek head. His fur wasn't
brown like the otters at Honeyvale
Wildlife Park, but a gorgeous light-
purple colour! "Hello," she murmured
to him. "You're very cute." He nuzzled

against her hand happily.

"Bright Eyes! Come back here!" gasped a voice and a nymph burst out of the bulrushes, shortly followed by another. They looked about the same age as Jasmine, Ellie and Summer, but they had pointed ears and their skin was a very pale green. They had long silver-blonde hair and were completely identical, apart from the fact that one had two flowers in her hair and the other only had one. They stopped rather shyly in front of the girls. The otter scampered back to them.

"Who are you?" Jasmine asked.

"Are you water nymphs?" Ellie asked curiously. The girls had met water nymphs before – they lived in water and were a bit like mermaids, except they had legs, not tails.

The girl with one flower nudged her sister. "Yes," the nymph with two flowers grinned. "We live in the Sapphire Stream and look after the riverbank and all the creatures that live here. I'm Clio and this is my twin, Halie."

"And this is our pet otter, Bright Eyes," said Halie shyly, crouching down and picking up the otter. He opened his mouth as if he was grinning at them.

Clio looked at their tiaras. "Are

you the special human friends of King Merry?"

"Yes," said Jasmine. "I'm Jasmine, and this is Summer and Ellie," she pointed to them each in turn.

"We thought you were!" said Halie. "Our cousin Nadia told us all about meeting you. She talks about you a lot!"

Summer, Ellie and Jasmine smiled as they remembered the friendly water nymph who had helped them when they were at Lily Pad Lake. Summer was about to ask how Nadia was when Clio grabbed her hand.

"Have you come here to help *us* this time?" Clio asked eagerly. "Our poor stream is almost all dried up!"

"It's all Queen Malice's fault," said Halie, her big blue eyes filling with tears. "She got the horrible trolls to build a dam across the stream and now all the animals and fish have had to find somewhere else to live, the butterflies and dragonflies have flown away and the plants are dying."

"That's awful," said Summer sadly.

"We'll try and help you," said Jasmine. "We really will." She hated

seeing the dried-up stream. "But we also need to try and find a missing jewel. It's a sapphire – a shining blue gem. Have you seen it?" She looked at the nymphs hopefully but they shook their heads.

"No," said Halie. "But one of the others might have. Why don't you come and meet them and we can ask?"

Clio nodded. "It's not really safe to be out here in the open. Queen Malice might arrive at any moment. Come with us. We'll take you to the others. They're in our secret clearing."

The girls followed the water nymph twins through the tall brown rushes, long stalks with brown oval-shaped seed pods on the top. Jasmine, Summer and Ellie rushed after Halie and Clio as they twisted and turned through the reeds.

It was hard work but at last they reached a clearing where the rushes had been woven into a large circle. Other water nymphs were bustling round it, some male, some female. They were dressed in blues and greens and had the same silvery hair and pointed ears as the twins. There were animals there too. The girls spotted more otters as well as little rabbits and fluffy water voles. The water nymphs were caring for the animals – feeding them, cleaning the sticky mud out of their coats with fresh water and drying them with soft leaves until their fur and feathers were dry and fluffy.

"We normally use this clearing for dancing," Clio said, looking round sadly.

"I never thought we'd have to hide here."

Summer reached forward and squeezed the nymph's hand.

"Everyone! These are King Merry's special friends!" announced Halie.

"And they need our help!" Clio added.

The water nymphs all stopped what they were doing and greeted the girls excitedly. A beautiful older nymph made her way through the crowd. Her silvery hair was caught back in a loose bun and her dress swept down to her feet.

"This is Ionie," said Halie. "She's in charge of us all. And this is Mara and Melita and Kai and…"

There were so many names it was impossible to remember them all! But everyone seemed very friendly. The nymphs smiled and hugged the girls, welcoming them to their home. A couple of them fetched some soft woven riverweed cushions and then everyone sat down in a circle.

"So, how can we help you, girls?" asked Ionie, curiously.

Jasmine explained all about King Merry and the missing jewels. "We have

to find the sapphire," she finished.

"And we need to set King Merry and Trixi free," added Ellie.

"We'll do anything we can," promised Ionie. "Has anyone seen a sapphire?" she called to the other nymphs.

But to the girls' disappointment, all the other nymphs shook their heads.

"It must be nearby," said Ellie. "Or the spellbook wouldn't have brought us here."

"Why is this place called the Sapphire Stream?" Summer asked.

"That's because the water is such a beautiful sapphire-blue colour," Ionie explained. "It would be a very good hiding place for a blue gem. Why don't we all go to the stream and have a look for it? Maybe one of us will find it if we all look around together."

"That would be really kind of you, thank you," Summer said, stroking Bright Eyes, who had sat down beside her. The little otter wriggled happily as she tickled him behind the ears. "And maybe we can help you too."

"We could try and break down the dam and make the stream flow again," suggested Jasmine.

"It's not that easy. Every time we go anywhere near it those horrid trolls chase us off," said Clio unhappily.

"They're so big and mean," said Ionie with a shiver.

The other nymphs nodded and looked scared. "We're scared of them," said one.

"We just don't know what to do," sighed Ionie. "All the animals, fish and insects here rely on us. We should be protecting them and their home."

Jasmine jumped to her feet. "We'll help you stand up to the trolls!"

Ellie and Summer jumped to their feet beside her. "Definitely!" they said.

"You have to stand up to bullies!" Jasmine exclaimed.

Ellie nodded. "If you all work together you can do anything!"

"And then you can make the stream beautiful again," Summer told them.

The nymphs looked at each other.

"Maybe we can," said Ionie uncertainly.

Jasmine reached down and pushed her finger into the mud beneath their feet. She wiped it on her cheeks in two lines like a soldier and put her hands on her hips. "You definitely can!"

she exclaimed. "From now on, Queen Malice and those trolls had better watch out!"

Queen Malice Takes a Dip

The girls and the nymphs set off towards the lake, with Bright Eyes and the other otters bounding ahead. But they hadn't been going for long when Bright Eyes came charging back. He sat up on his back legs and chattered frantically at them, his front paws waving in the air.

The nymphs all gasped.

"What is it?" asked Ellie.

"Bright Eyes says Queen Malice is by the pool!" whispered Clio.

Everyone looked at Jasmine. "Drop down onto your tummies!" she instructed them. "We'll crawl through the reeds and spy on her to see what's going on. Then we'll decide what to do." Her heart thumped with excitement.

Everyone crouched down. The girls stayed together. They crawled through the reeds like soldiers on a mission.

Summer thought how much her brothers would like to be there with them – it was like the game they had been playing in the wildlife park, only for real!

They spread themselves out around the dam until everyone was hiding in the reeds surrounding Queen Malice's bathing lake. Ellie and Summer smeared mud on their faces for camouflage like Jasmine had and then they cautiously lifted their heads. On the other side of the lake was a large black chair, resting on a little platform that was being carried on the shoulders of two large trolls. The panels and doors were decorated in gold, and fluttering from a flagpole at the back was a black flag with a gold thunderbolt streaking across it. Two Storm Sprites were perched on the top of the roof, their grey leathery wings folded back against their bodies.

The trolls holding up the chair looked horrible. Their bodies were big and lumpy and their arms hung down so their knuckles nearly rested on the floor. Their heads were huge, with bristly, green hair,

and their eyes were dark and beady like little pieces of coal. Each of them had a big wooden club strapped to his back. As the girls watched, the trolls put down the chair and one came round to open the door.

"Ready, Majesty?" he grunted.

"Yes, I am! Let me out right now!" The cold voice made an icy tingle run down the girls' spines. They knew that voice very well!

The troll opened the door and Queen Malice stepped out haughtily. She was tall and thin with frizzy, black hair and was wearing a long black dress and cloak. She had a pointed nose and in one hand she held a black staff. She looked round at the lake with a satisfied sneer. "I shall now take my bath, but first of all

I need a bathing costume. TRIXI!" Her voice rose to a screech and she jerked a gold chain that was tied to her wrist. "Trixi! Where are you, you lazy little pixie! Come and do my bidding!"

The girls caught their breath as a tiny pixie flew slowly out of the carriage. Her green leaf was attached to the other end of the chain and she was stood on it sadly. The girls knew she hated working for Queen Malice, but as a royal pixie she had to serve whoever was ruling the Secret Kingdom.

Trixi stood up and Summer gasped. Their little pixie friend usually wore colourful clothes made out of flower petals and leaves, but now she was wearing a tiny black dress just like Queen Malice's! As Summer watched,

Trixi pulled at her skirt crossly.

"Come on, you ridiculous little thing. I want a beautiful bathing costume and I want it NOW!" ordered the queen.

Ellie longed to jump up and tell Queen Malice to stop bossing Trixi around. She knew the queen could magic up her own bathing costume perfectly well, and was just being horrible.

"COME ON!" the queen shrieked, pulling the chain so violently that Trixi almost fell off her leaf.

Trixi seemed to think for a moment and then tapped the green jewel in her pixie ring.

"Pixie magic, from gem of green
Conjure a swimsuit fit for the queen!"

There was a flash so bright that Ellie blinked. As she opened her eyes again she saw that the queen was wearing an old-fashioned swimsuit that covered her arms and came down to her ankles. It was striped in black and grey and there was a matching bonnet that covered the queen's frizzy hair. Of course! It was a *horrible* swimming costume – just fit for a horrible queen!

Ellie looked at her friends and grinned.

Summer was shaking with laughter and Jasmine was going bright red as she tried not to laugh out loud.

Even Trixi looked as if she was trying to hide her giggles.

Ellie smiled. It was good to see that Trixi was still her old self, even if she did have to do everything Queen Malice said.

"What is this?" demanded Queen Malice, pulling at the stripy fabric on her legs.

"It's the latest fashion, Your Majesty," Trixi said innocently. "Everyone wants a bathing costume like that. They really do."

"Hmm." Queen Malice inspected herself in the surface of the pool. "Well, I suppose I do look good. Yes, yes, only the latest fashion for a queen like me!" She patted the hair that was poking out from under the bonnet. "Now, I shall bathe! Lilo! Drink!"

Trixi tapped her ring again and a black-and-gold lilo appeared, floating on the water. It had a back rest and a drink holder. The drink was in half a pineapple and had a gold cocktail umbrella and straw sticking out of the top.

"Storm Sprites!" the queen commanded. She held out her arms

and the two Storm Sprites stretched out their wings and flapped down from the carriage roof. They lifted her into the air and set her down on the lilo. The queen settled back and picked up her drink. "Dismissed!" she said, waving her other hand at them. Trixi's leaf was still attached to the evil queen's wrist and she had to hang on tightly as her leaf was pulled around.

"Queen Malice doesn't believe in saying please, does she?" Ellie whispered.

The others started giggling all over again.

"Ssh!" said Jasmine as Queen Malice started talking. *Maybe they would learn something about the jewels?*

"So..." the queen fixed Trixi with a beady look as the lilo floated out across the lake. "Have you found the gems yet?"

"No, Your Majesty," said Trixi, and the girls saw her quickly hide her delighted smile. "The trolls and Storm Sprites are looking, but no one has seen any sign of the royal jewels yet."

Jasmine, Summer and Ellie all breathed out in relief. They knew the emerald was safe, but it would have been awful if Queen Malice had managed to beat them to getting one of the other jewels.

The queen's expression darkened. "Well, *why* haven't they found them? Useless idiots! I want those jewels and

I want them NOW!" She yelled the last word and pulled the chain hard.

Trixi gasped and grabbed on to the sides of the leaf. "Well, you're not going to get them!" she cried bravely. "Jasmine, Summer and Ellie will find them and give them to King Merry and then he will become the ruler again. They'll do it. I know they will!"

Queen Malice spluttered angrily. "How dare you speak to me like that?" she screeched at Trixi. "I am the ruler of the Secret Kingdom and not even those interfering girls can stop me!"

Jasmine couldn't watch the queen bully Trixi any longer. "Oh, yes we can!" she yelled, bursting out of the bushes.

Ellie and Summer jumped up too.

"We'll get the jewels back for King Merry!" shouted Summer.

"You won't rule the Secret Kingdom for long!" yelled Ellie.

Queen Malice was so shocked that

her lilo overturned, and she landed in
the water with an enormous splash!
The watching nymphs and animals all
whooped and cheered.

When the queen surfaced, she had
lost her bonnet and her frizzy hair was
flat against her face. Water dripped off
her pointed nose. "YOU!" she shrieked,
pointing at the girls. "What are you
doing here? What—" She broke off and
then, suddenly, to the girls' astonishment,

the corners of her
mouth lifted
into a smile
and she
started to
laugh.

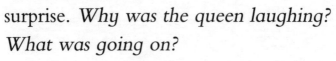

Ellie,
Summer and
Jasmine looked
at each other in
surprise. *Why was the queen laughing?
What was going on?*

"Ha! I know why you're here!" she
cackled in triumph. "It's because of the
jewels, isn't it? If you're here, it must
mean one of the royal jewels is hidden
around here too!"

Ellie felt as if her stomach had just filled
with cold ice.

Queen Malice began to wade through the lake towards the bank, pulling Trixi along like a balloon behind her. "Trolls! Sprites!" she screamed. "Destroy this place if you have to – just find me that jewel!"

⚜ The Jewel Hunt ⚜

The trolls started to bash through the reeds with their clubs. Queen Malice stepped out of the water and banged her staff on the ground, transforming her bathing costume back to her usual black dress.

"We've got to do something!" cried Jasmine in dismay. "They're destroying everything!"

All around them the water nymphs, rabbits, voles and otters were poking their heads up from their hiding places among the reeds. Ionie stood up. "The only way to stop them is to find the jewel before they do," she said quickly. "They won't rest until it's found. Come on, everyone. Help our friends. Get looking!"

The rabbits and voles bounded around the dam to the dried-up riverbed and started using their paws to push aside the mud, checking for any sign of the jewel. Summer ran to help them while Ellie started searching through the reeds with the nymphs. The otters rushed towards the lake and leaped into the water to search there.

Jasmine kicked off her shoes to rush

into the water with them, then stopped
as she realised she was fully dressed. If
only Trixi was there to magic *her* up a
swimsuit too...

Magic! As Jasmine thought the
word an idea came to her. Maybe the
spellbook could help? "Ellie!" she called.
"I need the spellbook!"

Ellie rushed out from the reeds and
pulled it out of her backpack.

"Look harder! Look faster!" Queen
Malice's harsh voice floated over from
nearby. The girls ducked into the reeds
as she passed, still shouting. "If you don't
find me that jewel, I'll lock you all in the
dungeons of Thunder Castle and throw
away the key!"

"What are you going to do?" Ellie
asked her friend.

"I need a swimsuit too!" Jasmine said as she started leafing through the pages. There were spells to change the weather, spells to make you fly, spells to fill plates with food...

Jasmine suddenly stopped at a page as she saw a clothes-changing spell. That might help! She just hoped the spell wouldn't give her a costume as silly as Queen Malice's!

She said the words out loud, then held her breath.

"Ancient Magic, please act with speed
And magic us up the clothes we need!"

There was a pop, and suddenly her clothes appeared in a folded up pile next to her and she found herself wearing a

stripy pink-and-white
swimsuit.

Jasmine
saw Ellie
gasp with
surprise as
her clothes
suddenly
changed
into a
costume
covered with
pretty purple
stars. Seconds later
Summer popped up in the grasses,
wearing a spotty yellow swimsuit. She
glanced over at Jasmine and Ellie in
astonishment and Jasmine held up the
spellbook. Summer nodded and smiled as

she realised what they had done.

As Ellie went back to hunt in the reeds, Jasmine hid the book safely with her clothes and then splashed into the lake. She was good at swimming underwater and she kicked her legs, diving deeper into the lake. Bright Eyes swam up alongside her and bumped his head encouragingly against her arm. Jasmine swam as deep as she could to try and check the bottom, but it went down a long way and she had to swim up to get some air.

As she reached the surface she could hear the Storm Sprites flapping overhead and the trolls crashing through the reeds. The water nymphs were calling out to each other.

"Have you found it?" one shouted.

"No, not yet!" another called.

"Keep looking!" the first one yelled.

Jasmine dived down again through the clear water, kicking hard. Her eyes

searched for any gleam or glint of the sapphire, but she still couldn't reach the bottom. It was too deep.

Just as Jasmine was about to give up and search somewhere else, Bright Eyes sped past her, his nimble body flipping and twisting easily though the reeds and his tail disturbing the mud as he searched. As the little otter swam by, Jasmine's heart flipped over. Next to Bright Eyes' tail, she spotted something glinting. Lying wedged between two big stones, almost invisible in the blue water, was a bright blue sapphire!

Jasmine stretched out as far as she could, but she just couldn't get down far enough to grab it. She surfaced, bobbing up next to where Clio and Halie were searching the mud by the dam.

Jasmine gasped for breath then waved at the nymphs. "Over here, twins!" she hissed, not wanting to attract the Storm Sprites' attention.

Clio and Halie jumped in and Jasmine whispered what she had found.

"We'll try and get it!" Clio offered. "We can usually reach the bottom of the stream if we use breathing reeds."

"What do you mean?" Jasmine glanced anxiously at Queen Malice. She didn't want the nasty queen to see them talking, but luckily she was too busy stomping about shouting orders at the Storm Sprites to notice.

"Look!" Halie swam to the bank and plucked a long reed. She put one end in her mouth and left the other end sticking out so she could swim underwater but still breathe. It was just like having a giant snorkel!

Halie swam down but the reed simply wasn't long enough. The water nymph couldn't get down much further than Jasmine could.

They all burst back out of the water together. "It's no good!" Halie whispered in frustration. "Usually we can reach the bottom of the stream with reeds, but

because of the dam the water is much deeper than usual."

Summer and Ellie had noticed Jasmine talking to the twins. They swam over to see what was going on.

"What's happening?" Ellie asked.

"We've found the sapphire, but we can't reach it!" Jasmine explained, pointing to the bottom of the stream.

"I'll try!" Ellie said. She dived down but she couldn't get to the bottom either. Even Summer had a go, although she wasn't quite as good at diving as the others were. But it was no good.

"Maybe Bright Eyes can help us," said Clio hopefully. She called to the otter and he swam over. She explaining what was going on in otter language, then Bright Eyes chirruped as if to say "Leave it to me!" and dived down into the lake.

Jasmine, Ellie and Summer ducked under the water and watched, but although Bright Eyes could reach the bottom he couldn't free the jewel from where it was wedged. His paws just weren't the right shape to wriggle down between the rocks and get the gem out.

"Oh, this is impossible!" said Clio as Bright Eyes surfaced beside her, chattering unhappily.

Halie hugged him. "You tried your best, I know," she comforted him. "Oh, if only the lake wasn't so deep at the moment."

"Hang on," said Ellie. An idea was forming in her head. "If we could make the lake shallower, then we could get the jewel, couldn't we?"

"Yes, but how can we do that?" asked Summer.

"We can break down the dam!" said Ellie. "Then the water will rush into the dried-up stream, the water level here will go back to normal and we can get the sapphire!"

"That's a brilliant idea!" Jasmine said.

"But we can't break the dam," Clio said. "It's too strong."

A smile spread across Jasmine's face. "No problem," she said, looking across at the huge, ugly trolls on the opposite bank. "We just need someone big and strong and stupid to break it for us – and I know just the people!"

Tricking the Trolls!

Ellie stared at Jasmine. She was sure she knew what she was thinking. "You mean we somehow trick Queen Malice's trolls into helping us?"

Jasmine nodded and grinned. "Ellie, Summer, come with me to the dam. Twins, tell everyone else to get out of the water and get ready for some action!"

The three girls swam over to the massive, towering dam. "OK, start talking about breaking it up," Jasmine whispered to Ellie and Summer. "And do it loudly!"

She started pulling at the wood and stones that made up the wall across the river. The others joined in.

"Come on! We've got to break this dam down!" Ellie called to Summer.

"I'm trying!" shouted Summer, tugging at a piece of wood and tossing it into the water.

"Keep your voices down, you two!" Jasmine said extra-loudly, pretending to look over her shoulder. "Don't let the trolls and Storm Sprites hear you, whatever you do!"

A sprite was flapping overhead. He

turned round sharply. "What are you
girls up to?" he screeched. "Quick! Trolls!
Get over here!" he shouted to two of the
trolls who were lumbering around near
the edge of the lake.

He flew down to the dam and two

trolls appeared at the water's edge, swinging their clubs. Summer gulped. They were very big!

"What are you doing, you pesky girls?" the sprite demanded, his beady eyes fixing on them.

"Nothing!" said Jasmine innocently. "We're just having a nice little swim."

"Oh, yes," Ellie joined in. "Enjoying the lovely clear water. We're not touching the dam at all."

"No, not at all," Summer added.

The sprite scowled. "You can't trick me. You're looking for the jewel. I know it!" His eyes suddenly widened. "You think it's in the dam!" he crowed.

"It's in the dam," grunted one of the trolls, pointing at the dam with his club. "Let's knock it down!"

"Bang. Crash!" said the other troll eagerly. "Let's do it!"

They lifted their clubs up.

"But there's no jewel in there," said Jasmine honestly.

"Definitely not," said Summer, hiding her grin.

The trolls lowered their clubs miserably.

"No jewel," said the first troll in disappointment.

"No bang and crash," said the second troll, his shoulders sagging.

"Ignore the girls! They're just trying to trick us!" said the sprite, his beady eyes gleaming. "They know the jewel is there! Knock the dam down."

"Oh, please don't!" said Jasmine. "We really don't want you to!"

"Jasmine's right – don't!" said Ellie,

stifling her giggles.

"Do it now, trolls!" shouted the sprite.

The two trolls needed no more
encouragement. They roared in delight
and lifted their clubs. The girls swam
out of the way just in time as the trolls
brought their clubs crashing down on the
huge dam.

"Queen Malice!" shrieked the sprite,

flapping up and down. "The jewel is over here in the dam, we're sure it is!"

"The jewel!" crowed the queen in delight. "Where is it? Let me see!"

Dragging Trixi's leaf after her, Queen Malice rushed over to the dam. The first sprite shrieked to the other sprites and trolls to come and help. They all raced over and started tearing the dam apart. Even

Queen Malice helped, blasting the rocks with her thunderbolt staff.

Trixi shot the girls a very worried look as she held on to her leaf tightly. Jasmine winked at her and the little pixie's face brightened with relief. She must have guessed that they had a plan!

Water started trickling through the holes in the dam and into the stream on the other side.

"Quick, we have to get out of the water," Ellie realised. "We don't want to be in here when the dam breaks!"

"Faster!" shrieked Queen Malice to the sprites and trolls. "Break it down!"

The three girls swam to the bank and climbed out. They were only just in time. Urged on by Queen Malice, one of the biggest trolls pulled out a massive boulder that was right in the centre of the dam.

All at once the water rushed through

the hole and suddenly, with a massive
CRASH, the dam collapsed! The air
was filled with shrieks and screams and
roars as Queen Malice, the trolls and the
Storm Sprites tumbled over and over in
the rush of water.

"HOORAY!" shouted the nymphs as
the water burst through the dam and the

stream on the other side refilled.

"The trolls wanted bang and crash," giggled Ellie. "I guess they got it!"

"And now *we* can get the sapphire!" said Jasmine.

She looked round. Because the stream was flowing properly again, the water was already much shallower. She should be able to reach the sapphire. She plunged from the bank into the water and dived down.

It was murkier in the water now because the flood had disturbed the mud at the bottom, but as she blinked she could just see a glint of blue between two rocks. She felt with her fingers. It was a tight fit. She prised and pulled, then her heart flipped with delight as the gem popped free. She rose back to the surface,

kicking hard. She had the jewel! They'd
found it at last!

"I've got it!" she cried without
thinking as she burst out of the water.

The sunlight fell on
the sapphire in
her hands and
it glinted and
glittered.
Jasmine
gasped
as Queen
Malice
turned
towards her. She
hid the jewel, but it
was too late.

"No!" the queen shrieked. She strode
up the riverbank towards Jasmine, her

clothes dripping wet, her face dark with fury. "Give me that jewel!"

Jasmine looked round in alarm. What should she do? The trolls were getting to their feet and lumbering after Queen

Malice, and the Storm Sprites were shaking the water off their wings and flapping towards her like giant bats. She couldn't run away from all of them!

Suddenly she heard a chattering noise. It was Bright Eyes! His head was poking out of the water next to her. He held out his paw and she understood. She quickly dropped the jewel into the water and watched as he scooped it up with his little claws. With a swish of his thick tail he dived down and swam away.

Ellie and Summer splashed into the water and stood beside Jasmine.

"Don't worry, we're here," gasped Summer.

"You're not going to face them all on your own," said Ellie.

"I want that jewel!" Queen Malice

yelled again, wading around the bits of broken dam.

"Well, you can't have it!" said Jasmine showing her empty hands. "It's gone."

"WHAT?" shrieked the queen.

"I don't know where it is now," Jasmine said truthfully.

Queen Malice screamed in rage. "Right! That's it! I'm going to turn you all into…" She raised her hands, then looked over at where her thunderbolt staff was resting on the bank. For a moment she faltered, then her gaze flew to Trixi and she gave a wicked smile.

"Pixie!" she cried. "I command you to do some more magic for me. I want you to turn these annoying girls into… into stink toads!"

Trixi paled. "No, Queen Malice!"

The girls exchanged anxious glances.

"You must do as I say. You're a royal pixie, aren't you? So you have to obey

me!" snapped the queen.

Trixi looked from
the girls to
Queen Malice
helplessly.
"I…um
…I…I
can't think
of anything
that rhymes
with stink
toad," she
said desperately.
"I can't do the spell!"

"Just do some magic!" shrieked Queen
Malice. "And do it NOW!"

Trixi reluctantly lifted her finger to tap
her pixie ring.

Summer grabbed Ellie's and Jasmine's

hands and held on tight. She knew their pixie friend had no choice – she was going to have to turn them into stink toads!

Standing Together

Trixi looked at Queen Malice, her eyes suddenly sparkling. "All right!" she declared in her silvery voice. "I'll do your spell!" She tapped her ring and called out:

"My queen is here to stop your fun..."

Queen Malice cackled in delight and rubbed her hands together expectantly. Trixi shot her a triumphant look.

"Ellie, Summer, Jasmine…RUN!" Trixi finished.

The girls gasped as they felt their feet begin to run. They splashed out of the stream and into the bulrushes, faster than they had ever run in their lives. Behind

them they heard Queen Malice shriek with rage.

"NOOOOOOO!"

The girls ran into the bulrushes and crouched down to hide. The water nymphs crept over to them. "You did it!" whispered Ionie. "You saved our stream!"

"Look!" said Clio. The girls glanced round and saw that the nymphs were right. Now that the stream was flowing again, all the reeds and rushes had turned from brown to green. Butterflies were fluttering over the water and dragonflies swooped about, their blue bodies glinting like jewels as their wings whirred.

Rabbits were hopping along the banks and the water voles were running in and out of their burrows while the otters played tag in the water. The stream was as beautiful as it had looked when they'd first seen it in the spellbook.

"Thank you so much!" said Halie, hugging the girls.

"But where's the sapphire?" said Ionie.

Jasmine smiled. "I think I know," she said. She explained how she'd passed it to Bright Eyes. The clever otter would be taking it somewhere really safe – the clearing!

"But what are you going to do about Queen Malice and her trolls?" said Ellie. "What if they try to build the dam again? What will you do?"

Ionie threw back her shoulders. "We won't let them! You've shown us all that we have to be brave. If we stand together, not even Queen Malice can defeat us. Go and find the sapphire, girls," she added softly. "And we will deal with Queen Malice." She reached down and put her hands in the mud then wiped stripes across her cheeks and across Halie's and Clio's. "It is time for us to be brave like you!" Then she turned and raised her fist high above her head. "Nymphs! River creatures!" she shouted. "Follow me! We must get rid of our enemies. Charge!"

Whooping and shouting, the nymphs charged into the stream and ran across it towards the trolls and sprites, who were gathered around Queen Malice and the black carriage. The otters bounded along with them and all the animals on the banks charged too.

Queen Malice froze. "What…what's happening?"

But her voice was drowned out by the yells and shouts of the water nymphs as they splashed through the water, waving their arms fiercely.

The queen picked up her skirts and jumped into the carriage. "Quick!" she shrieked. "Get me out of here!"

"With pleasure, Your Majesty!" cried Trixi. She waved towards the bulrushes, then called out a spell:

"The queen is filled with terror and
fear.
Pixie ring, take us away from here!"

There was a green flash and Queen
Malice, her Storm Sprites and trolls
vanished! The water nymphs cheered
with delight.

"I think that's the last the water
nymphs will see of Queen Malice!" said
Jasmine in relief.

"Trixi's so clever and brave," said
Summer. "I hope she doesn't get into
trouble for helping us."

"We must find the jewels as fast as
we can so she won't have to work for
Queen Malice any more," said Ellie.
"Where's the sapphire?"

"I think it might have been taken

this way," said Jasmine. She led them through the bulrushes until they reached the water nymphs' secret clearing. Sitting in the centre of it was Bright Eyes. He chattered happily when he saw them and bounded over. With a big otter grin, he held out his paws and showed them the brilliant blue sapphire.

"Thank you, Bright Eyes," Jasmine said, taking the jewel and stroking him. "Thank you so much."

Summer crouched down and the little otter jumped on her lap, reaching up to snuffle at her cheek. She kissed the top of his head. "You're very clever, Bright Eyes." He gave her a cheeky look and nibbled at one of her bunches.

Jasmine looked at the glittering blue gem. "We must keep this safe until we find all the other jewels."

"Let's go and tell King Merry we've found it," said Summer.

"First we'll need the spellbook," said Jasmine. "Wait here!" She ran back to the stream and picked up their clothes and the spellbook, then rushed back to the clearing. After they'd changed their clothes, Summer found the travelling spell that would take them to the dungeon in Thunder Castle where King Merry was being kept prisoner.

"Remember we need to say where we want to go," Ellie reminded the others. "So on the third line, all say 'castle dungeons'!"

Jasmine and Summer nodded. Ellie held up the book and they all said the spell together.

"Ancient magic, take us swiftly
Far away through time and space.
Carry us to the castle dungeons
And set us in the safest place."

As they said the last word, the girls felt themselves being whirled away.

They spun round and round until their
feet hit a stone floor. They opened their
eyes and found themselves in the dark,
miserable corridor outside King Merry's
cell. The gloom was lit only by a couple
of candles in spiky black holders, but
inside King Merry's cell there was a

light shining brightly. The girls ran to the door and looked in. The king's cell looked just as cosy as when they had last seen him. There was a soft rug on the floor, a light with a spotted lampshade, an armchair with squishy cushions, a table and a big comfy bed. Two plates covered with big silver domed lids were on the table and the king was snoozing in the armchair, his hands folded across his rounded tummy and his half-moon spectacles perched on the end of his nose as he snored.

"King Merry!" Summer called softly. "King Merry! It's us!"

The king gave a start. He looked round and almost fell off the armchair in surprise. "Goodness gracious me! Crowns and sceptres! How lovely to see you all."

He jumped up and pushed his spectacles
further up his nose as he came over to
the door. "Does this mean…have you
found… Oh, you have!" he exclaimed
in delight as Jasmine pulled out the blue
jewel and held it up.

"We've found the sapphire, King Merry. And we helped everyone at Sapphire Stream at the same time."

"Oh, well done, girls!" King Merry clasped his hands together and did a little jig. "You're magnificently marvellous! Just wonderful!"

Ellie grinned. "We saw Trixi too. She's all right, but Queen Malice keeps bossing her around."

"Are you OK, King Merry?" asked Summer anxiously.

"Oh, don't worry about me, my dear.

I'm as right as rain!" the king said. "It's not much fun being stuck in here, but I have every comfort I could need – a bed, a comfy chair, delicious food…"

He lifted one of the silver lids and a big pie with steaming vegetables magically appeared. He put the lid back on and then lifted the other to show them a massive ice cream with an umbrella and crown-shaped sparkler stuck in the top. "I just wish I could leave this dungeon and deal with that horrible sister of mine. I hate the thought of everyone in the kingdom being so unhappy."

"We'll get you out soon," Summer said sympathetically.

"Yes," Jasmine added. "We've only got two more royal jewels to find and then you'll be the ruler of the Secret Kingdom once more!"

"You won't be in here for much longer," Ellie promised.

"Thank you, my dear girls," beamed King Merry.

Ellie glanced down at the book in her hands. "Let's ask the finding spell to look for the next royal jewel now!"

The girls crowded round the spellbook and flicked to the right page. The first two lines of the finding spell were there:

"Something's lost that must be found,
Search through sea, air and ground..."

But there was nothing more.

"When the spellbook finds the next jewel, the rest of the spell will appear." said King Merry. "But for now, it is time for you to go home."

"We'll be back as soon as we can,"
Jasmine promised.

"Bye, King Merry!" Summer said. "See
you soon."

"Travel safely," said the king. Then
he scrunched up his face like he was
remembering something. "Oh! Before
you go—"

He took the ice cream and put the
silver lid back on the plate. He waited
a second and lifted it. A perfect little
birthday cake was sitting there with
pink-and-white icing and a single silver
candle already twinkling. The king
smiled at Summer. "Happy birthday, my
dear!"

"How did you know?" Summer said,
blushing pink with pleasure as she took a

deep breath and blew out the candle.

King Merry tapped his nose. "Aha, I know many things." He carefully sliced the cake and passed the pieces though the bars. Summer, Ellie and Jasmine took a piece each and nibbled them happily. Summer had never had birthday cake in a dungeon before!

When they'd finished, Ellie licked her fingers clean and picked up the spellbook. "We'd better go," she said. "We've got lots more birthday fun waiting for us at home."

Summer and Jasmine nodded. "We'll be back as soon as the spell finds the next jewel," Summer promised King Merry.

Ellie turned the pages until she reached the going-home spell. She looked at the others. "Ready?" Ellie read the spell out:

"Our quest's complete,
Our journey's done.
Take us home: Three, two, one!"

The spell lifted them up and twirled them away. Faster and faster they went until they were finally set down gently in the woodland park behind the bench where they had started out. No time had passed in the real world – it never did while they were in the Secret Kingdom.

"This is definitely a birthday I'll never forget!" said Summer. "The Secret Kingdom...nymphs...otters...seeing King Merry..."

"*And* getting to defeat Queen Malice and a load of ugly trolls!" said Jasmine.

"A perfect birthday!" grinned Ellie.

Just then, Finn came running towards them.

"They're here, Mum!" he shouted over his shoulder. He beckoned to the girls. "Mum and Dad have said we can go and get ice creams. We're allowed three scoops each. Come on!"

"I'm still full of King Merry's cake!" Summer whispered to her friends.

"There's always room for ice cream!" Jasmine declared. "I want chocolate sprinkles on mine!"

"Mmm, and strawberry sauce!" Ellie agreed with a grin.

Summer glowed with happiness. She

knew there was still lots to do before the Secret Kingdom was back to normal, but they'd found another jewel, her best friends were with her and they were about to have huge ice creams. "I wish every day was my birthday!" she said with a smile.

**Join Jasmine, Ellie and Summer
in the next Secret Kingdom
adventure,**

Read on for a sneak peek...

A New Spell

Ellie, Summer and Jasmine were sitting
on the grass by the duck pond, breaking
up the crusts from Ellie's leftover
sandwiches. Their schoolbags lay beside
them on the grass.

Four ducks swam in circles, quacking
hopefully. "Here you are!" called
Summer, throwing in the bits of bread.

The ducks dived and squabbled for the crusts.

Jasmine laughed as she copied their quacks. One of the ducks looked at her and quacked back. "I can speak duck!" said Jasmine, quacking again. "He's saying, 'Thank you very much, please may I have some more?'"

Ellie grinned at Summer. "Jasmine's gone quackers!"

Summer giggled as Jasmine gave Ellie a playful push.

"I wonder if any other animals live around this pond – animals that keep themselves hidden like water voles or otters," said Jasmine, looking round.

"Not otters," Summer said right away. She knew lots about animals. "They prefer moving water, like rivers."

Ellie checked no one was nearby. "Like the Sapphire Stream," she whispered. The girls exchanged smiles. The Sapphire Stream was a beautiful stream in the Secret Kingdom where water nymphs and lilac-coloured otters lived!

"I wonder if the Secret Spellbook has found out where the last two jewels are yet?" said Jasmine. The girls looked at each other and sighed sadly.

The Secret Kingdom was usually an amazing place, but recently it had been taken over by evil Queen Malice and a gang of ugly trolls. The queen had locked her brother, kind King Merry, in one of the dungeons at Thunder Castle and was trying to rule the kingdom! But she couldn't become the proper ruler until she found four gems that were usually hidden on the inside of King Merry's crown. Before Queen Malice had stolen the crown, King Merry had cast a spell to protect it. As usual, the little king's spell had gone a bit wonky and the four royal jewels – an emerald, a sapphire, a ruby and a diamond – had disappeared and hidden themselves around the kingdom. If Jasmine, Summer and Ellie could find the jewels and return them to the king, then a new crown would form and King Merry would become the ruler again! So far, the girls had found the emerald and the sapphire.

"Where is the spellbook at the moment?" Summer asked.

"In my ballet bag back at home," replied Jasmine. "I checked it before school this morning but it still hadn't found the next jewel."

The Secret Spellbook was a book of ancient, powerful spells. It was trying to track down the missing jewels for the girls. Whenever it found out where a jewel was, a new spell would appear in the book – and the girls could use it to take them to where the jewel was hidden!

Read

༄Diamond Wings༄

to find out what
happens next!

Secret Kingdom

Have you read all the books in Series Five?

Queen Malice has taken over the Secret Kingdom! Can Ellie, Summer and Jasmine find all the royal jewels and make King Merry rule again?

Secret Kingdom

Keep all your dreams and wishes safe in this gorgeous Secret Kingdom Notebook!

Includes a party planner, diary, dream journal and lots more!

Out now!

Secret Kingdom

Catch up on the very first books in the beautiful Secret Kingdom treasury!

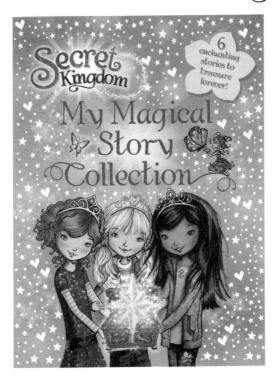

Contains all six adventures from series one, now with gorgeous colour illustrations!

Out now!

Secret Kingdom

Be in on the secret.
Collect them all!

Series 1

When Jasmine, Summer and Ellie discover
the magical land of the Secret Kingdom,
a whole world of adventure awaits!

Sugarsweet Bakery

ROSIE BANKS

Bubble Volcano

ROSIE BANKS

Dream Dale

ROSIE BANKS

Lily Pad Lake

ROSIE BANKS

Midnight Maze

ROSIE BANKS

Fairytale Forest

ROSIE BANKS

Series 2

Wicked Queen Malice has cast a spell to turn King Merry into a toad! Can the girls find six magic ingredients to save him?

Secret Kingdom

Series 3

When Queen Malice releases six fairytale baddies into the Secret Kingdom, it's up to the girls to find them!

Code Breaker

King Merry needs your help! Can you break the code to help him remember what he's scared of?

A	B	C	D	E	F	G	H	I

J	K	L	M	N	O	P	Q	R

S	T	U	V	W	X	Y	Z

_____ _____

Secret Kingdom

A magical world of
friendship and fun!

Join the Secret Kingdom Club at

www.secretkingdombooks.com

and enjoy games, sneak peeks and lots more!

You'll find great activities, competitions, stories
and games, plus a special newsletter for
Secret Kingdom friends!